W9-BOL-666

ATHENEUM BOOKS FOR YOUNG READERS

An imprint of Simon & Schuster Children's Publishing Division

1230 Avenue of the Americas, New York, New York 10020

Click, Clack, Moo: Cows That Type

text copyright © 2000 by Doreen Cronin

Click, Clack, Moo: Cows That Type

illustrations copyright © 2000

by Betsy Lewin

Giggle, Giggle, Quack

text copyright © 2002 by Doreen Cronin

Giggle, Giggle, Quack

illustrations copyright © 2002 by Betsy Lewin

Dooby Dooby Moo

text copyright © 2006 by Doreen Cronin

Dooby Dooby Moo

illustrations copyright © 2006 by Betsy Lewin

All rights reserved, including the right of

reproduction in whole or in part in any form.

ATHENEUM BOOKS FOR YOUNG READERS is a registered trademark

of Simon & Schuster, Inc. For information about special discounts

for bulk purchases, please contact Simon & Schuster Special Sales

at 1-866-506-1949 or business@simonandschuster.com.

The Simon & Schuster Speakers Bureau can bring authors to your

live event. For more information or to book an event,

contact the Simon & Schuster Speakers Bureau at 1-866-248-3049

or visit our website at www.simonspeakers.com.

Book design by Ann Bobco

The text for this book is set in ITC American Typewriter.

The illustrations for this book

are rendered in brush and watercolor.

Manufactured in China

0610 SCP

First Edition

2 4 6 8 10 9 7 5 3 1

CIP data for this book is available from the Library of Congress.

ISBN 978-1-4424-1263-7

The stories contained herein were originally

published individually.

Doreen Cronin

A Barnyard Collection

Click, Clack, Moo
and
more

illustrated by
Betsy Lewin

Atheneum Books for Young Readers

New York   London   Toronto   Sydney

Greetings from the Barn

Betsy Lewin sure looks innocent enough when she shows up, but don't let her fool you—she's the one that let Duck loose! It's been ten years since we breathed life into the troublemaking Duck, who can wield a typewriter, a pencil, a microphone, a campaign speech, and a pair of night-vision goggles with equal aplomb. I'm not sure Betsy or I anticipated the affection that young readers would have for Duck, but I'm so glad they did! I hope that children see that it's okay to cause a little trouble now and then—it keeps the grown-ups (and Farmer Brown) on their toes!
—D. C.

From the moment I read *Click, Clack, Moo*, I knew the barnyard gang, and Doreen, would become family. Ten years later my affection for all of them has not waned, and I never tire of sharing all these books with children.
—B. L.

CLICK, CLACK, MOO
Cows That Type

For my Dad —D.C.
To Sue Dooley —B.L.

CLICK, CLACK, MOO
Cows That Type

Farmer Brown has a problem.
His cows like to type.
All day long he hears

Click, clack, **moo.**
Click, clack, **moo.**
Clickety, clack, **moo.**

At first, he couldn't believe his ears.
Cows that type?
Impossible!

Click, clack, **moo.**
    Click, clack, **moo.**
Clickety, clack, **moo.**

Then, he couldn't believe his eyes.

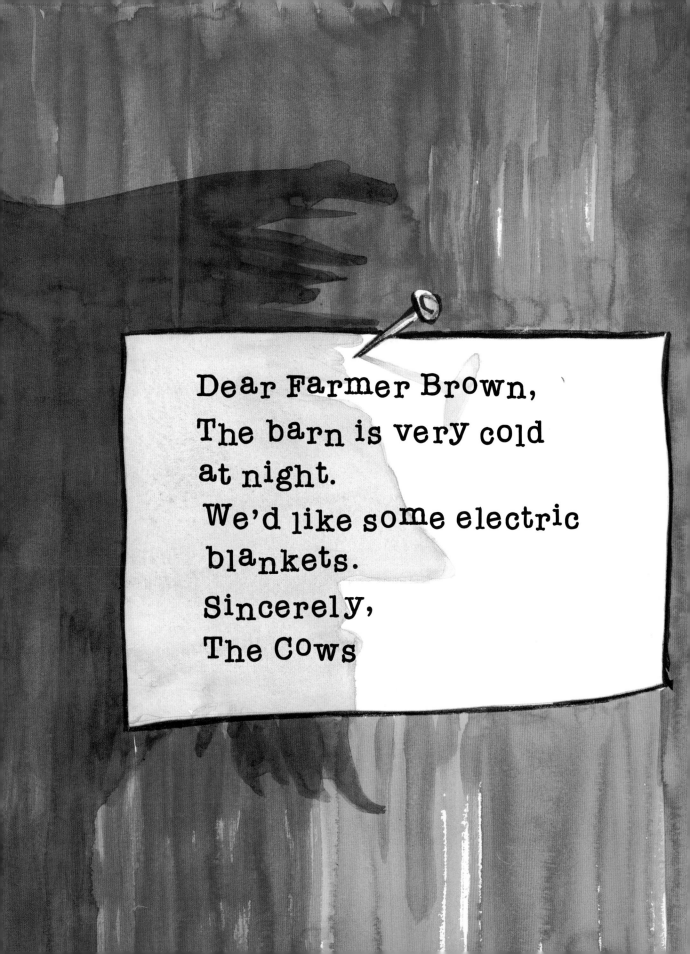

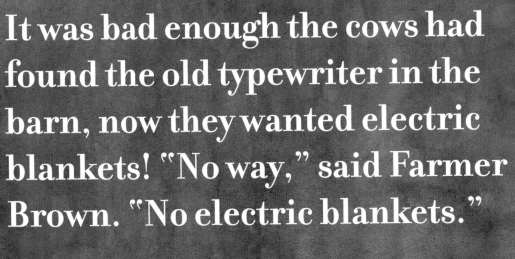

It was bad enough the cows had found the old typewriter in the barn, now they wanted electric blankets! "No way," said Farmer Brown. "No electric blankets."

So the cows went on strike. They left a note on the barn door.

"No milk today!" cried Farmer Brown. In the background, he heard the cows busy at work:

Click, clack, **moo.**
Click, clack, **moo.**
Clickety, clack, **moo.**

The next day, he got another note:

Dear Farmer Brown,
The hens are cold too.
They'd like electric
blankets.
Sincerely,
The Cows

The cows were growing impatient with the farmer. They left a new note on the barn door.

"No eggs!" cried Farmer Brown.
In the background he heard
them.

Click, clack, **moo.**
   Click, clack, **moo.**
Clickety, clack, **moo.**

"Cows that type. Hens on strike! Whoever heard of such a thing? How can I run a farm with no milk and no eggs!" Farmer Brown was furious.

Farmer Brown got out his own typewriter.

Dear Cows and Hens:
There will be no electric blankets.
You are cows and hens.
I demand milk and eggs.
Sincerely,
Farmer Brown

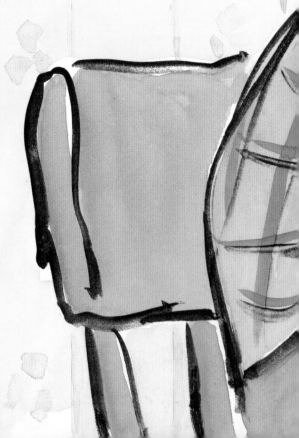

Duck was a neutral party, so he brought the ultimatum to the cows.

The cows held an emergency meeting. All the animals gathered around the barn to snoop, but none of them could understand Moo.

All night long, Farmer Brown waited for an answer.

Duck knocked on the door early the next morning. He handed Farmer Brown a note:

Dear Farmer Brown,

We will exchange our typewriter for electric blankets.

Leave them outside the barn door and we will send Duck over with the typewriter.

Sincerely,
The Cows

Farmer Brown decided this was
a good deal. He left the blankets

next to the barn door and waited for Duck to come with the typewriter.

The next morning he got a note:

Dear Farmer Brown,
The pond is quite boring.
We'd like a diving board.
Sincerely,
The Ducks

Click, clack, **quack.**
Click, clack, **quack.**
Clickety, clack, **quack.**

Giggle, Giggle, Quack

For Andrew
—D. C.
For Rosanne Lauer
—B. L.

Giggle, Giggle, Quack

Farmer Brown was going on vacation. He left his brother, Bob, in charge of the animals.

"I wrote everything down for you. Just follow my instructions and everything will be fine. But keep an eye on Duck. He's trouble."

Farmer Brown thought he heard
giggles and snickers as he drove
away, but he couldn't be sure.

Bob gave Duck a good long stare
and went inside.
He read the first note:

Giggle, giggle, cluck.

Twenty-nine minutes later
there was hot pizza in the barn.

Bob checked on the animals before he went to bed. Everything was just fine.

Wednesday is bath day for the pigs. Wash them with my favorite bubble bath and dry them off with my good towels. Remember, they have very sensitive skin.

Giggle, giggle, oink.

Bob had all the pigs washed in no time.

Farmer Brown called home on
Wednesday night to check in.
"Did you feed the animals like
I wrote in the note?" he asked.

"Done," replied Bob, counting seven empty pizza boxes.

"Did you see my note about the pigs?"
"All taken care of," said Bob proudly.

"Are you keeping a very close eye on
Duck?" he asked.

Bob gave Duck a good long stare.
Duck was too busy sharpening his
pencil to notice.

"Just keep him in the house," ordered Farmer Brown. "He's a bad influence on the cows."

Giggle, giggle, moo, giggle, oink, giggle, quack.

Thursday night is movie night. It's the cows' turn to pick.

Giggle, giggle, moo.

Bob was in the kitchen, popping corn. Just as the animals settled in to watch THE SOUND OF MOOSIC, the phone rang.

The only thing Farmer Brown heard on the other end was:

"Giggle, giggle, quack, giggle, moo, giggle, oink. . . ."

UH-OH.

"DUCK!"

screamed Farmer Brown.

For Mom
—D. C.

To Claire Rose Reilly
and Logan Patrick McMurray
—B. L.

Farmer Brown keeps a very close eye on his animals. Every night he listens outside the barn door.

Dooby, dooby moo . . .
the cows snore.

Fa la, la, la baaaa . . .
the sheep snore.

Whacka, whacka Quack . . .
Duck snores.

Duck keeps a very close eye
on Farmer Brown.

Every morning Duck borrows
his newspaper. One day,
an ad catches his eye:

TALENT SHOW!!!

OPEN TO ALL!!

where: COUNTY FAIR
when: SATURDAY

1st prize: A TRAMPOLINE!!*

2nd prize: BOX OF CHALK**

3rd prize: VEGGIE CHOP-O-MATIC

* Slightly used. Sponsor makes no warranty, expressed or implied, nor assumes any responsibility in the use of the trampoline.

** Actual amount awarded will be based on availability.

As soon as Farmer Brown opened his paper, he knew the animals were up to something.

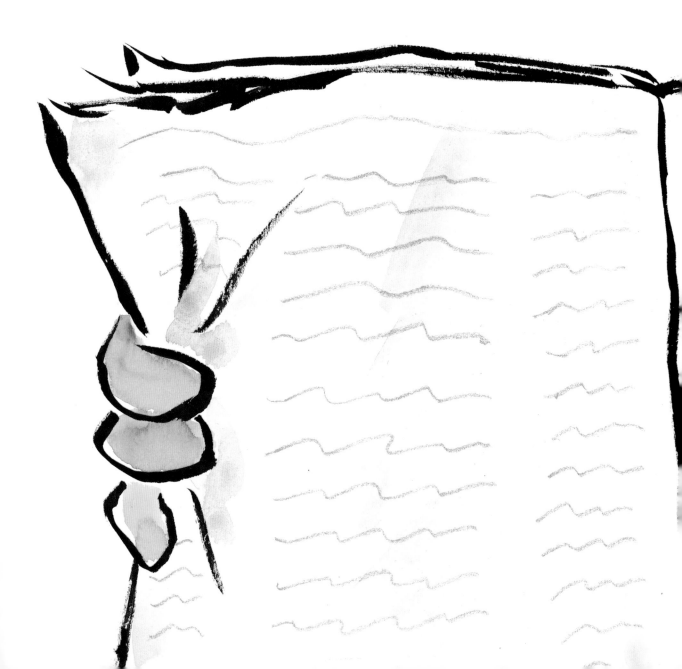

Farmer Brown watched them closely all day.

He watched them
from above.

He watched them from below.

He even watched them upside down.

Outside the barn, late at night, he heard,

Dooby, dooby moo . . .
Fa la, la, la baaaa . . .
Whacka, whacka Quack . . .

Inside the barn, the cows rehearsed
"Twinkle, Twinkle, Little Star."

Dooby, dooby, dooby moo.
Dooby moo, moo, moo, moo, moo.

Needs work, Duck noted.

The sheep rehearsed
"Home on the Range."

Baaa, baaa, baaa, baaabaaa.
Fa la baaa, fa la baaaa, baaaabaaabaaa!

Duck had them try it again,
with more feeling.

The pigs did an interpretive dance.

whacka, whacka

quaaack . . .

snored Duck.

Day after day, Farmer Brown kept a very close eye on the animals.

He watched from the left.

He watched from the right.

He even watched in disguise.

Outside the barn, night after night, he heard:

Dooby, dooby moo . . .

Fa la, la, la baaaa . . .

Whacka, whacka quack . . .

Inside the barn, night after night,
the animals rehearsed.

Finally it was time for the county fair.

Duck was
pacing
back
and forth.

The pigs were combing their hair.

The cows were drinking tea with lemon.

They ARE up to something!
thought Farmer Brown.

Farmer Brown
was not going
to leave them alone.

He loaded all the animals into the

back of his truck and drove to the fair.

When he got there he heard:

Dooby, dooby moo . . .

Fa la, la, la baaaa . . .

Whacka, whacka quack . . .

He parked his truck and headed off to the free barbecue.

When Farmer Brown was out of sight, the animals ran to the talent show desk and signed in.*

Cows
Sheep
Pigs

* Contestants consent to the use of his/her name, photograph, and/or likeness for advertising and promotional purposes in connection with this promotion without additional compensation, unless prohibited by law.

The cows sang
"Twinkle, Twinkle, Little Star."

Dooby, dooby, dooby moo.

Dooby moo, moo, moo, moo, moo.

Two of the judges were clearly impressed.

The sheep sang "Home on the Range."

la, la baa.

ba, ba, baaa, baa, ba, baaaa.

Three of the judges were clearly impressed.

It was time for the pigs' interpretive dance.
But they were sound asleep.

Shloink oink, oink, oink, oink.

All of the judges were clearly annoyed.

Duck really wanted that trampoline.
He jumped on stage and sang
"Born to Be Wild."*

QUack, QUack, QUuuaaaaaaCKK!

The judges gave him a standing ovation.

* Original words and music by Mars Bonfire

When Farmer Brown got back to the truck,
he heard:

Dooby, dooby moo . . .
Fa la, la, la baaaa . . .
Whacka, whacka QUack . . .

The animals were exactly where he had
left them.

That night Farmer Brown listened
outside the barn door.

Dooby, dooby BOING!

Fa la, la, la BOING!

Whacka, whacka BOING!

The events and characters depicted in this picture book are fictitious.
Any similarity to actual persons, living or otherwise, is purely coincidental.